This book is dedicated to the memory of
Mayumla Tsering Wangmo (1923-2022).

For generations in Tibet her family (the Lakar family),
were benefactors of many monasteries and sponsored
all kinds of dharma activities.

She was the mother of four children, including
Sogyal Rinpoche and Dzogchen Rinpoche, and
was renowned as a great dakini. She was the sister
of Khandro Tsering Chödrön and the daughter of
Dechen Tso, the princess of Ling.

Mayumla spent the last twenty years of her life living
at Lerab Ling, a Buddhist retreat centre in France.

HAVE YOU EVER BEEN TO LHASA?

Written and illustrated by Samuel Horwood

Every year Emma's mother liked to go on holiday to a meditation centre on the top of a hill, in the middle of nowhere.

Emma's mother liked to meditate.

Emma did not like to meditate.

Emma liked beach holidays where she could ride waterslides, or she liked clothes shopping in malls and sometimes horseriding.

It was the school holidays, and once again Emma found herself at the meditation centre on the top of a hill in the middle of nowhere - not joining in activities with a bunch of other children, whose parents were also off practicing their meditation.

Emma was sitting on the edge of the group sulking. She had decided that at ten years old she was far too old for the childish activities she was being asked to join in with, and her Mum should really have taken her to Florida, which was where she had wanted to go on holiday.

Welcome to FLORIDA

At lunchtime Emma's Mum (Sarah) came to collect her. Tashi (a Buddhist monk) said "Hello Sarah. Emma's been very patient, but I think she's a little bored - why don't we all go and get lunch together!"

They began walking off together. Emma, her Mum and Tashi down along the track to the dining hall, when out of nowhere a white car glided past them and came to a stop.

"It's Mayumla" Tashi said as he opened the door. Sitting there was a small, smartly dressed, elderly Tibetan lady with big bright eyes shining out of her kind face. "She's going for her daily outing and wants us to join her. Jump in, it will be fun!"

Emma and Sarah got in either side of Mayumla. She looked at them with big sparkly eyes full of magic and smiling said "Da drag can gyi mthar sbyar rgyu slar bsdu'i phrad cig ...Da Lhasa?" in a gentle quiet voice.

Emma had no idea what Mayumla had just said. Tashi said "Oh yes, Mayumla only speaks Tibetan - no English. She just asked you if you have ever been to Lhasa?"

"Where is Lhasa?" asked Emma as the car began to smoothly and quietly drive off, almost as if it were floating.

Emma was not very tall and from her window seat she couldn't see the ground, soon a cloud appeared curiously close to her window, she peered out and could see the meditation centre far below 'We're flying' she thought to herself as they entered a big fluffy cloud and everything went white.

They began to float down out of the cloud and Emma could see huge, snow capped mountains much bigger than she had ever seen before. Soon she could make out little villages, temples and fields as they flew down towards a wide green valley with a turquoise coloured river snaking through it. They landed softly in a lush green meadow.

"Ah Tibet!" Mayumla said as they got out of the car. "I haven't been here for so long." Emma was surprised as she realized she was now able to understand what Mayumla had said, but she was even more surprised to see that Mayumla was now a beautiful young Tibetan princess.

"Where are we and what's going on?" Emma whispered to her mum through gritted teeth as she took in the huge valley they were standing in.

"Not quite sure darling" her mum replied excitedly, "but Mayumla and Tashi will take care of us I'm sure."

"Look, a tent" Tashi said pointing at a camp not far away. "Let's go and say hello".

Mayumla sang folk songs as they walked through the long grass towards the camp and she occasionally picked one of the flowers that covered the meadow like thousands of little jewels.

"These are my favourite" Mayumla said to Emma holding up a bright yellow flower.

"That's called a buttercup!" Emma said.

"A butter cup – what a funny name. You just gave me an idea" said Mayumla "a cup of real Tibetan butter tea would be very nice. Have you ever had butter tea Emma? It's very popular in Tibet."

"Never" replied Emma.

A trail of smoke wound its way slowly out of a hole in the top of the tent, which was criss-crossed with prayer flags[1]. Clothes had been hung out to dry over the tent ropes and there were horses and yaks happily grazing on the meadow grass.

1 A Tibetan prayer flag is a colorful rectangular cloth, often found strung along trails and peaks high in the Himalayas. They are used to bless the surrounding countryside and for other purposes.

Two children, a girl and her younger brother came running to greet them. "Tashi delek!²" they said when they arrived.

"Tashi delek! These are for you" Mayumla said and placed two pretty flower necklaces she had made over their necks.

"Tuk-je-che!³" the children said smiling, looking down at their new necklaces, "come and have some butter tea with us." "Well, what an auspicious invitation" Mayumla said as they each took her by the hand and led her inside.

Inside there was a stove with pots and pans bubbling away on it warming up the whole tent. Woolen rugs covered the floor and walls, there were cupboards, a table and a shrine, which had a big picture of a young smiling Dalai Lama.

The children's parents were there getting ready to have tea. They both looked at their unusual guests curiously before saying "Tashi-delek, please sit down." The children's mother had long woven pigtails and necklaces made out of large round egg-yolk yellow beads.

They all sat on the floor around the table with their steaming butter tea.

Emma smelt the tea and it was like butter that had gone off. Maybe it tastes better than it smells she thought lifting the mug up to her mouth and taking a sip of the tea. "Yuk, that tastes disgusting" she said out loud, making everybody laugh.

"Emma!" her mum said, "that's not polite."

2 Tashi delek is a Tibetan expression used in greeting, congratulation, and good-luck wishes.
3 'Thank you' in Tibetan

"No problem" the father laughed, "children why don't you take Emma outside and show her where this disgusting tea we love so much comes from."

As they went outside together Emma asked them "Do you like it here? don't you get bored? There's nothing here!"

"We love it! Our parents teach us about our way of life so that we can take care of ourselves when we get older and sometimes we help with chores and to pack up when we move camp. But most of the time we have this whole valley as our playground."

They pointed at the hairy yaks with their big horns happily munching on the long green grass "The milk for the tea comes from yaks milk. Come and meet Pema she's my favourite. We give all of our animals names."

"Tashi-delek Pema" they both said patting her firmly. Pema blew out of her nostrils with a "hrrmpph" in a pleased to see them kind of a way.

"She gives us milk and we make butter and cheese out of it. You can pat her if you want, she loves the attention." Emma stroked Pema's thick outer hair.

"In the summer we cut her hair and use it to make ropes and also the fabric of our tents. Underneath this outer hair is soft wool." The girl took Emma's hand so that she could feel the soft woollen hair underneath. "With this we can make clothes and blankets that keep us very warm and cosy."

"We also use their poo!" the little boy chimed in cheekily.

"Yes it's true we use it on the fire as fuel to heat our tent and to cook, so really the yaks provide us with everything we need."

As they wandered back to the tent their father was strapping patterned blankets and saddles on to three horses. Two were shiny chestnut coloured that looked like they had white socks on and the third was a magnificent white horse.

"This kind man has offered to lend these horses to us so that we can ride to Lhasa" Mayumla told Emma as she put her foot in the stirrups and got up onto the white horse. "I like this one. You can come with me, it will be quicker than walking and a lot more fun!"

Before she had time to argue the man helped Emma up onto the white horse in front of Mayumla as Emma's mum and Tashi got on to their horses.

"Tuk-je-che" they said to their new friends, "We'll be back tonight" and with that they galloped off in the direction of Lhasa.

FINE
FOODS

BUT
T

"It's so good to be back in Lhasa" Mayumla said with a smile as they trotted along the back streets. There were lots of shops, markets, restaurants and food stalls giving out delicious smells and especially vendors selling momos[4]. The streets were full of people, there were groups of monks and nuns young and old, traders and pilgrims walking around spinning prayer wheels or holding malas[5]. Some of the women had incredible hairstyles and were beautifully dressed with layers of intricately decorated clothing and necklaces made out of amber, turquoise and coral beads. Young children with thick black scruffy hair ran around playing, there were poor people begging and old Tibetans with wrinkly tanned faces and not many teeth that smiled at them as they rode past.

"I'm starving, let's get something to eat, I know a great place - come on!"

At the restaurant the cooks were busying themselves putting fillings into small circles of dough, which they would close up and place in steaming pans. "Tashi delek" they said while rolling momos, stirring soups and broths and making long thick noodles.

4 Tibetan dumpling
5 Buddhist prayer beads

"Please come in" the waiter said as she held open the curtain to the restaurant. The walls of the restaurant had detailed paintings on them depicting Tibetan fairytales. Red lamps hung down to light each table, even the ceiling had intricate patterns painted on it. They were seated at a quiet table in the corner with comfortable cushions.

The waiter clapped her hands and two more waiters immediately came out carrying trays covered with different dishes, which they arranged quickly and precisely on the table.

"Best momos in Lhasa – what do you think?" Mayumla asked Emma and her Mum as she dipped a momo in some sauce.

Emma was stuffing another of the momos into one half of her mouth, but managed to say "Delicious" out of the other half.

When they had eaten until they could eat no more, the waiters cleared away their empty dishes and they leaned back on the cushions completely happy and content.

"Right you both need something to wear, you need to blend in a bit more. We're going to do my second favourite thing, chuba shopping!"

They left the restaurant thanking the waiters and the cooks and soon arrived in a street full of clothes shops.

"Here it is" Mayumla said. The sign above the shop read 'Mr. Wangchuk's boutique, the finest chubas in Tibet'.

A yak's bell clanged as they opened the door to the shop, inside was magical – it smelt of incense and the walls were full of beautiful brocaded dresses from sky blue, to pink, to turquoise and violet, deep blue to scarlet red, as well as black and different golden colours. In the patterns decorating the chubas Emma was able to make out lotuses, tigers, birds, mountains and clouds.

"Decorated silks from the finest tailors in Tibet and China" Mr. Wangchuk said smiling as he came out to greet them.

Mayumla helped Emma and Sarah to try on some chuba's. First they put on beautiful silk shirts, then the main dress, which was very colourful and decorated with lotuses. They had to help each other to tie the small ties at the back of each others dress.

They both came out of the dressing room to ooh's and aah's from Mr. Wangchuk. "What beautiful dakinis[6]" he said, "do you like them?"

Emma loved the smooth silk chuba with all the textiled decorations "Yes, very much" they both said.

'We'll take them!' Mayumla told him.

---

[6] Dakini' is a female embodiment of enlightened energy and is translated as 'sky-goer', indicating one who traverses the 'sky' of the expanse of wisdom.

Mr. Wangchuk was very happy that he had sold two chubas and picked up a 'dramyin', a Tibetan folk instrument that looks like a small guitar.

"Do they know how to dance" Mr. Wangchuk asked Mayumla as he started to pluck the strings rhythmically.

"Like this" Mayumla started stepping in time to the music and moving her arms, "copy me."

"And copy me too" Tashi said as he began jumping around, the sight of which Emma and her Mum found so funny that they joined in too. Mayumla began to sing in time to the music. She sung a very high-pitched fluttering melody as they all danced together in Mr. Wangchuk's chuba shop.

As they were saying goodbye to Mr. Wangchuk there was a deep, haunting sound that echoed all the way across the city. Mayumla told Emma "That is the sound of the Potala Palace monks blowing on long trumpets from a cliff way up above Lhasa. It lets everybody know that there is going to be an event in the Potala temple. Do you want to go?"

"Okay.. whats the Potala Palace?" Emma asked?

"It's where the Dalai Lama lives!" Tashi replied.

They rounded a bend and were awestruck by an incredible view of the magnificent Potala Palace rising above the city. It was built on top of one steep hill overlooking Lhasa. It had steps that zigzagged up to the golden temple roofs at the top and Emma couldn't help wondering what was in all of those rooms and behind all of those windows and would have liked to have been able to spend time exploring them.

They tied their horses up near a wall where lots of Tibetans were walking alongside and spinning a golden pray wheel as they passed it.

"These people are making koras around the palace. A kora is when you circumambulate around a sacred site."

"Circum-what?" said Emma.

"Cir-cum-mam-bu-late, it means walk all the way around. These people are walking around the Potala Palace. It can be like a meditation or a pilgrimage and each of these prayer wheels has thousands of printed meditation chants wrapped up inside it, so that when you spin one it is said to have the same effect as if you were reciting all of these chants at once."

"Ready for some exercise?" Mayumla shouted down at them as she began nimbly climbing the palace steps at a speed which was not easy to keep pace with.

As they reached the temple near the top of the palace they could hear deep loud chanting from the monks inside and there were clouds of white incense smoke billowing out from something that looked like a large chiminea.

Emma turned around to look at the view, she could see right across the city and tried to spot the momo restaurant and Mr. Wangchuks chuba boutique. It felt like she was standing on top of the world.

The temple pillars were coloured red and gold, with lots of rainbow coloured carvings and paintings. There were golden dragon faces at the top of the pillars and also Emma could see flowers, clouds and beautiful golden script. Above the grand entrance doors were carvings of elephants, roosters and monkeys and at the top there were fierce looking snow lions[7].

Inside the temple rows of monks of all ages sat facing each other leaving a corridor in the middle, which led to a huge smiling golden Buddha. Underneath the Buddha was a teacher in a red robe sitting on a throne. The monk leading the chanting was big and chubby with a deep, rich voice that welled up from deep inside him. Sometimes he would chant very slowly and powerfully, at other times he said the words very quickly.

7 The Snow Lion is a celestial animal of Tibet. It is the emblem of Tibet, representing the snowy mountain ranges and glaciers of Tibet, and may also symbolize power and strength, and fearlessness and joy. It is said to represent unconditional cheerfulness, a mind free of doubt, clear and precise. Two snow lions feature on the Tibetan national flag.

The atmosphere felt magical and powerful, but at the same time Emma felt very cosy. After such an eventful day her thoughts began to settle and she started taking in her surroundings. The monks sitting in the front rows were playing traditional Tibetan instruments which included high pitched wind instruments, cymbals and big round drums and at certain points they would crash and bang them noisily. During all of this the teacher sat on his throne as still as a statue. He gazed out at the monks and people gathered but he didn't look at anything in particular. He appeared to be relaxed and in command, 'like a king' thought Emma.

She felt a tap on her shoulder "Chai?" A monk was holding out a wooden bowl for Emma. "Do you want some chai tea, very sweet, very delicious?" Emma was unsure, but the tea smelt very nice so she took a cup and the monk filled it up with steaming tea. "Thank you" Emma said warming her hands on the hot cup. 'This is nice' she thought to herself, 'sitting in front of the Buddha drinking a nice cup of tea – cheers!' and the Buddha looked like it started to smile even more.

After a short while the monks stopped playing their instruments and quickly chanted some prayers as everybody else begun to queue up to receive a blessing. The teacher would touch them on their heads and greet them as if he were meeting an old friend.

Mayumla had two beautiful white scarves decorated with symbols[8] that she gave to Emma and her Mum saying "offer this with your hands together." When the teacher saw Mayumla his eyes lit up "How are you? Tashi-delek!" He took the scarf that she was offering him and put it back around her neck and then they touched their foreheads together.

"Tuk-je-che, I am very well Rinpoche[9]. I would like you to meet my friends Emma and her mother Sarah."

The teacher looked so powerful and important and yet he was also very gentle and friendly. Emma felt her heart fluttering in her chest, surprised at how excited and nervous she was to be meeting the teacher.

"Oh, Tashi-delek Emma and Emma's mother" the teacher said as he put the white scarves back around their necks. "Very nice to meet you" and he lovingly placing his hand on each of their heads. "I do hope you are having a lovely visit and that Mayumla is taking good care of you."

"Oh yes, she really is" Emma replied excitedly.

He signalled to his attendant to give something to him. The attendant handed him two red cords with knots tied in them. The teacher blew onto both knots and he tied them gently around their wrists. "These cords are to remind you of your trip to Lhasa, I hope you come back one day and we can see each other again."

They left the temple and went outside into the bright light of day and were surprised to see a huge rainbow arcing from one side of the city to the other.

8 The eight auspicious symbols: The Most Precious Parasol. The Auspicious Golden Fishes. The Wish-fulfilling Vase of Treasure. The Exquisite Lotus Blossom. The Conch Shell of Far Renown. The Glorious Endless Knot. The Ever-Flying Banner of Victory. The All-powerful Wheel.
9 Rinpoche literally translates as 'precious one'. An honorific title accorded the seniormost lamas of the Tibetan Buddhist tradition.

"Well, how auspicious!" Mayumla exclaimed. They all stood there marvelling at the sight of this and feeling very happy at having had such an exciting adventure. The rainbow slowly dissolved and Mayumla patting Emma on the head said "I think it's time we headed back, I hope it wasn't too boring for you Emma?"

Emma just giggled.

They climbed down the palace steps and up onto their horses and galloped out of Lhasa.

Leaving the horses to have a good feed they thanked the family profusely for their kindness.

The car was waiting where they had left it and they got in and drove off, floating up above the green meadow and their friends' camp, above the valley with the turquoise coloured river snaking through it, over the mountains and into a big white cloud.

"Wake up Emma!"

"What" replied Emma as she sleepily opened her eyes.

"You slept through the whole drive" her mum told her. "We've arrived back and Mayumla and Tashi need to go, so say goodbye to them."

Mayumla gave Emma a mischievous smile and waved to her as they drove away. She was back to being the kind elderly Tibetan lady, Emma had first met.

As Emma lifted up her hand to wave goodbye she felt something and noticed a red cord around her wrist. She reached down to touch it and remembered a wonderful dream she had had about visiting Lhasa with Mayumla as a young princess.

Mayumla as a young woman.

Printed in Great Britain
by Amazon